ARCTIC
AESOP'S
FABLES

Twelve Retold Tales

Susi Gregg Fowler ❄

Illustrations by Jim Fowler

SASQUATCH BOOKS
SEATTLE

To my grandchildren, Callahan Jon and Cedar Lillyanny.
Your creativity inspires me. —sgf

To my brother-in-law Keith,
for your generosity and compassion. Thank you. —jf

Manufactured in China by Midas Printing International Ltd. (Hong Kong), in November 2012.

Published by Sasquatch Books

17 16 15 14 13   9 8 7 6 5 4 3 2 1

Editor: Gary Luke

Project editor: Nancy W. Cortelyou

Illustrations: Jim Fowler

Design: Sarah Plein

Library of Congress Cataloging-in-Publication Data is available.

ISBN-13: 978-1-57061-861-1

Sasquatch Books

1904 Third Avenue, Suite 710

Seattle, WA 98101

(206) 467-4300

www.sasquatchbooks.com

custserv@sasquatchbooks.com

WITHDRAWN

The Wolf and the Reflection

A wolf, wandering alone on the tundra, was feeling a little hungry when his keen nose told him there was food nearby. Following the scent, he found a nice, meaty bone. Perhaps a bear had left it behind, but "finders, keepers" is the rule of the wild, and the wolf was grateful for something to fill his belly. A cozy hollow among the grassy tussocks on the other side of the river would be just the right place to enjoy his meal.

As he leaped from rock to rock across the river, the wolf glanced down. There, looking up at him, was another wolf—and that wolf had a bone, too. It looked as if the other wolf's bone had more meat on it than his. Outrageous! He was determined to get that bone for himself.

Of course, the other wolf was simply his own reflection, and the other bone was just a reflection also. Too bad the poor, greedy fellow didn't see this.

The jealous wolf braced himself and jumped off the rock into the water. He snapped at the other wolf as he jumped, and as he did so, dropped his bone. The reflected wolf and bone disappeared in the splash, and the river swiftly carried the real bone out of reach.

Climbing out of the water, the wolf shook himself, grumbling because he was back where he started—only now he was wet as well as hungry.

Moral: Gratitude for what one has fills a body better than envy over what one has not.

The Butterfly and the Caribou

A caribou stood nibbling the grass growing up through melting snow. Ahhh. It tasted good. Summer comes late in the Arctic, and it had been a long and bitter winter. The caribou was grateful for the change of seasons and an increase in available food. He and the rest of his herd had already journeyed a long way from their winter range. As they headed toward the Arctic coastal plain, he could almost taste the approach of summer in these late spring grasses.

A butterfly flew by and settled down to rest on one of the branches of the caribou's new antlers. After a while, the insect was ready to fly off again, but before he did so, he cleared his throat.

"Excuse me, but will you mind terribly if I leave now?" the butterfly asked, fluttering his beautiful wings.

The caribou huffed and snorted in amusement. "I had no idea you were even there, silly," he said. "I certainly won't miss you when you go."

Moral: We are not always as important as we may think.

The Bat, the Birds, and the Beasts

Long ago, the birds and the beasts of the Arctic fought each other in battle after battle in a struggle to determine who were the true leaders of the North. Sometimes the beasts won, led by the mighty bears, the wolverines, and the caribou. Sometimes the birds won, led by the fierce peregrine falcons, the eagles, and the owls.

The bat was a little fellow. Even then, there weren't many bats in the Far North, so perhaps he had reason to be so cowardly—for cowardly he was. He simply couldn't decide whose side he was on. Did he belong with the birds, who seemed to own the skies? Or did he belong with the mammals, who commanded the land?

All the bat knew for sure was that he wanted to be one of the winners, so he chose first one side and then the other, depending on who claimed the day's victory. He wildly cheered the winners and loudly booed the losers.

In time, the birds and beasts tired of their endless battles.

It turned out to be a foolish way to pass time that would be better served by gathering food, building homes, caring for young, or even sleeping.

Once the fighting ended, the creatures turned their attention to the fickle bat. They remembered the way he had switched sides. They remembered how he had laughed at them when they were losing. And they were determined to teach him a lesson he wouldn't forget. But how? Everyone was tired of fighting, and they did not really want to harm the bat. So they held a council and came up with a plan.

All the birds and beasts who had once fought so furiously against each other gathered in a giant circle. They brought the bat into the center of this circle of fur and feathers, and, as one, they began to laugh. They laughed and they laughed, and then they laughed some more. The bat was so embarrassed that he fled the light of that bright Arctic sky forever. Poor little bat.

Moral: The pretense of friendship is no friendship at all.

The Arctic Fox and the Raven

A raven squatted in a scrawny black spruce, a big chunk of fish in her beak. She had snatched this piece of grayling from someone's catch left on the riverbank. "Hee hee. How brave and clever I am," she thought. "Truly, in all ways a remarkable bird."

Along came an Arctic fox, his fur just starting to change to its winter white color. "Foolish fellow," the raven thought. "He looks quite scruffy trotting along, nose to the ground. He probably doesn't even realize I'm here." But the raven was quite wrong about that.

The fox stopped under the spruce and glanced at the raven. That piece of fish looked mighty tasty, but he knew better than to imagine the raven would willingly part with it. He would have to be sly.

The fox spoke to the raven. "Oh, what do my eyes see?" he said. "You are a beauty, madam."

"Hmmm," thought the raven. Perhaps the fox was not as foolish as she first thought.

"Your black feathers gleaming in the sun dazzle my eyes," the fox went on. "I am curious to know whether you move as elegantly as your appearance suggests. If so, you would surely be the most beautiful bird in the North."

Pleased, the raven shifted from one foot to the other, circling around and ruffling her feathers, looking as proud as a bird with fish dangling from her beak possibly could.

Clapping his front paws, the fox said, "Oh, madam. I am overcome by your gracefulness."

The raven bowed.

"Your eyes shine like the sun, and your movement is a dance," continued the fox. "I don't suppose it is possible that your voice could match your looks and grace in splendor. If it did, I would demand that you be proclaimed queen of all the creatures in the Arctic."

The flattered bird could not resist showing off her fine, scratchy caw. "Kaww," she called—and, as she opened her beak, the piece of fish tumbled to the ground, where the Arctic fox gobbled it up.

It was mighty tasty, too.

Moral: Do not trust a flatterer—and beware your own vanity!

The Bear, the Wolves, and the Musk Oxen

One day a hungry grizzly bear came upon a herd of musk oxen wandering the tundra, chewing on grasses and small plants. Grasses and plants were not the kind of food the bear was hungry for. A musk ox, though—that was more like it.

The bear carefully watched the musk oxen, with their long, shaggy hair. *Oomingmak*, "the animal with skin like a beard," is what the Inupiat Eskimo people named them. Yes, one of those bearded animals would make a fine feast.

And so the grizzly headed for the nearest musk ox. Slightly apart from the rest of the herd, she looked to be an easy mark for a powerful hunter like him. But as the bear approached, there was a sudden rumble of hooves as all the other musk oxen ran to the side of the animal the bear had already thought of as his dinner. The musk oxen formed a line facing the bear—and they did not look like they wanted to play Red Rover.

The bear turned tail and ran off to seek easier prey.

Hungry must have been the mood of the day, for before long, a pack of wolves approached the musk oxen. They had observed the grizzly's failure. Too bad for the bear, but as they knew, wolves in a pack have an advantage over an animal hunting alone. The musk oxen could protect themselves from any single attacker,

but wolves would surround the line, attacking from behind as well as from the front.

The wolves began to lope across the plain toward the musk oxen, who raised their heads from their chewing and moved toward each other. The wolves began to separate, some one direction, some the other. They could almost taste musk-ox meat.

This time, though, the musk oxen did not form a line. Instead, they formed a tight circle, these *oomingmak*. They stood shoulder to shoulder in a ring, all facing out, their calves safe inside the ring. Now, wolves are brave, but none of them wanted to leap straight into the horns of those large beasts standing in their circle of protection. So, the wolf pack, too, left disappointed.

And if those musk oxen had not stood together? Now, that would have been a different story, with a very different ending.

Moral: United we stand.

The Raven and the Jar

A raven, wings black and shiny as oil, circled a jar the people had left behind on their way to fish camp. Too bad for them but good for the raven, for down in the bottom of that jar, there was a little bit of water.

It had not rained for many days, and the raven was thirsty. Now, he could have flown to the river—plenty of water there—but this fellow was feeling a little lazy. He was happy where he was, except for his thirst. And now there was water in sight.

The raven stuck his beak into the jar. He could almost smell the water, but either the jar was too tall or the raven's beautiful beak was too short. However you want to look at it, the raven couldn't get to that water.

The thing about ravens, though, is that they don't give up easily.

Looking around, the raven spied a pile of stones. He picked up a stone in his beak and dropped it into the jar. Picked up another and dropped it, too. And then another. The water in the jar rose a little with each stone. He dropped another stone and another and still another until, finally, the water rose enough to meet the thirsty raven's beak. He drank the water down to the very last drop. Ahhh.

Moral: Necessity is the mother of invention.

The Crab and His Mother

Walking along the edge of an Arctic shore, a mother crab noticed the strange way her son was walking. "Why are you shuffling sideways?" she scolded. "March straight ahead. It's up to our family to set standards for all the other crabs. Do not embarrass me."

The young crab tried to walk forward, but failed. His mother was practically hopping up and down in frustration. If you have seen an irritated crab, you know why cranky people are often called "crabby."

"Do it again," insisted the mother crab. "You're just not trying hard enough!"

The unfortunate crab did try, but all he could accomplish when moving forward was a slow stumble.

"I can't," he said finally. "Perhaps if you show me, I will be able to copy you."

"Oh, for goodness' sake," snapped his mother. "I'll do it, then. Now, watch and learn."

But as she tried to move forward down the beach, the mother crab found herself stumbling just as badly as her son. Puzzled, she tried again, with the same result. Indeed, the proud mother crab had never paid particular attention to the way she walked. She was astonished to realize that she also walked sideways—and for perfectly good reason. Moving quickly required bending the joints on her legs—but they only bent sideways. Who knew!

"Well, obviously, sideways is just as good," she said. "In fact, it's much better this way. Those creatures moving forward down the beach look ridiculous. Thank goodness we are crabs—and crabs walk sideways." And off they scooted together, mother and son, scuttling sideways, into the surf.

Moral: Practice what you preach, and do not demand of others what you cannot do yourself.

The Hare and the Porcupine

The poor little porcupine is so slow that were it not for her quills, any number of beasts would be delighted to have her for lunch—and not as a guest.

The snowshoe hare is a small creature, only a fraction of the size of a porcupine, but oh, can he run.

Every time the porcupine and the snowshoe hare met up, the hare bragged about his speed and made fun of the porcupine. "You're so big and round, it's amazing you ever get anywhere."

The porcupine was a solitary creature, content to mind her own business, munching leaves and wandering wherever her feet took her. Surely, she thought, if she just ignored the hare, he would get tired of his teasing. But it didn't work.

"You couldn't escape an enemy if your life depended on it," the hare jeered. "You'd be in someone's belly already without those quills. No great loss, either."

Well, even a porcupine's patience does not last forever. Finally, she had had enough.

"You may be fast," she told her tormenter, "but I am steady. I believe I could even beat you in a race. What do you say to that?"

Why bother asking! The hare knew that with his large hind feet and lean body, he was made for speed. Race the porcupine indeed. Still, when the porcupine quietly repeated her challenge, the hare was forced to accept. It would be good for a laugh, anyway.

The day of the race arrived, and the snowshoe hare and the porcupine met at the start of the agreed-upon course. Ready, set, go!

The hare laughed as he leaped past the porcupine. Eager to put her in her place, he began running circles around his slow-moving competition. The porcupine ignored his antics,

however, and the hare grew bored and raced on ahead.

When the hare came to a clump of dwarf Arctic willow, he looked back. He noted smugly that the porcupine was far behind him. Why not stop for a little nibble? Hmmm, yes. He did enjoy an afternoon snack.

Full and satisfied, and with the sun beating down on him as hot as ever it gets in the Arctic, the hare decided a little nap would be nice. He looked back again, and the porcupine seemed no closer than she'd been before, so he found a sheltered spot, lay down, and fell sound asleep.

Meanwhile, the porcupine lumbered on, ignoring the tender leaves and flowers on her way. "Victory will taste sweeter than these," she thought, and with great determination she continued toward her goal. Like the hare, she felt the heat of the sun, but her will was strong. She passed the sleeping hare and kept on toward the finish line.

At last, the porcupine saw the other animals, waiting for their first glimpse of the snowshoe hare. Imagine their amazement when the porcupine came waddling into sight instead.

As the porcupine padded across the finish line, there was such a loud cheer that it awakened the hare. He bounded up from his dreams and ran as fast as his legs would carry him. Too late. Feeling more than a little foolish, the snowshoe hare followed the porcupine's trail and crossed the line.

And the only one who wasn't surprised by the way things turned out? Why, the porcupine, of course.

Moral: The race is not always to the swift, but to those who keep on going. Slow and steady wins the race.

The Arctic Ground Squirrel and the Sandhill Crane

The Arctic ground squirrel heard the sandhill cranes coming before she saw them. The cranes' rolling cry was unmistakable, and the squirrel didn't think it fair that not only did they get to fly far away every year, but they had glorious voices that filled the air with a wondrous, musical rattle. The squirrel was tired of her own "sik sik" voice. She was tired of the sounds of the rest of her colony. And she was really tired of only seeing her own patch of the Arctic. She longed for travel and adventure.

The squirrel's complaints became her only conversation. Why should the birds have all the luck? Why was she not born with wings? Why shouldn't she see the shoreline of Southeast Alaska or the valleys of California? Why could she not fly above the earth?

The sandhill cranes settled down in the tundra near the squirrel, but they grew so irritated by her constant complaints that at last one of them offered to take her up into the sky. The crane's beak looked a little threatening to the squirrel, but to everyone's relief, she decided to accept the crane's offer. At last she would dance with the clouds.

Picking up the squirrel with his long black toes, the crane lifted into the air. The two flew almost to the clouds. At first, the squirrel thrilled to the joy of flight. But the crane kept on flying, up and up, until the land was so far below that the squirrel could barely see her home—and still the crane kept flying. The air up high was cold, and the crane's claws were sharp. And the squirrel started to get hungry. How was she going to eat up here? This wasn't fun anymore. The squirrel called to the crane, but her squeaks faded in the vastness of the sky.

She looked down again. The tundra—her home—looked so beautiful. How had she not noticed its beauty? It spread out, a vast plain with tiny patches of color: caribou moss, saxifrage, clumps of willow, bearberries, and more. On the land she could stretch her legs and run around, nibble willow leaves, and chase other squirrels. Oh, what she wouldn't give to be back on the ground, running about on her own four feet. Flying was for the birds!

Suddenly, the ground was coming closer and closer. The sandhill crane was gliding down to rejoin his companions. Just before landing, he loosened his grip on the squirrel. She tumbled over twice as she landed, but picked herself up and raced back to her colony without even a thank-you or a good-bye.

With the wonderful earth under her feet, the Arctic ground squirrel couldn't imagine a nicer place to be, and raised her voice to call to her companions. "I'm back! Sik sik!"

Moral: Be careful what you wish for.

The Hungry Wolverine and the Hare

Hungry. Hungry. Hungry. This was the chant of the wolverine out hunting one day in late winter. A lemming came into view—not a great meal, but better than only the memory of food. Just as the wolverine prepared to snatch up the lemming, she caught sight of an Arctic hare. Why bother with a few mouthfuls when the hare, almost half the wolverine's size, would really fill her empty belly? The wolverine decided to wait for the hare to come close enough to catch.

Now! The wolverine leaped—but not quite far enough. The hare bounded right past her. The wolverine followed, but the hare, almost invisible against the snow, soon disappeared from view. The wolverine, recognizing defeat, gave up the chase. This time, she would just have to be satisfied with the lemming.

Poor hungry wolverine. She now discovered that the lemming, too, had disappeared. If only she'd eaten it when she'd had the chance.

Hungry. Hungry. Hungry. Greed is a risky business.

Moral: Pie in the sky is a poor substitute for food in the belly.

The Mosquito and the White-Fronted Goose

A mosquito buzzed along an icy stream. She was just one of the many mosquitoes who swarm throughout the Arctic in the summer and delight in biting the hides of Arctic mammals. A sudden puff of wind blew her into the water, where a white-fronted goose floated in the sunlight. The goose opened her beak to snap up the mosquito, but paused when she heard a tiny voice.

"Spare me, please," begged the mosquito. "If I can, I will do you a favor one day."

Preposterous! Nonetheless, the goose scooped the mosquito onto her beak and set her on the bank. The mosquito quickly dried in the sun and flew off, calling, "Thank you. I won't forget this, and I will help you if I can."

Shaking her head at such foolishness, the goose headed back to her nest on the ground, where her mate and their goslings, six fluffy balls of feathers, waited.

Toward evening, the adult geese went off together to get food, secure in the knowledge that the goslings were safely tucked out of sight. The pair had no idea that a hungry Arctic fox had discovered their nest. The fox planned to snatch some goslings for supper, but he didn't want to tangle with the parents, who weighed almost as much as he did. No, he intended to stay far from the threat of their flapping wings and sharp beaks. He would wait until the pair were far enough from the nest that they couldn't reach him before he escaped with his feathery meal.

Shhh! It was almost time. Silently and swiftly, the fox crept toward the nest, gauging the right moment to grab the goslings. The geese never even looked his way. But someone else saw him.

Ouch! Something pricked him right on his tender nose. Ouch! It pricked him again. The fox was so startled that he jumped. His jump alerted the goslings, who started squeaking. And at that sound, the mother goose and her mate turned and raced back just in time to protect their babies. The hungry Arctic fox escaped, but without any supper.

The mother white-fronted goose recognized the mosquito buzzing past her. "Thank you," she called as the tiny insect disappeared from view. The little mosquito had, indeed, been true to her word.

Moral: One good turn deserves another. And remember that small friends can do great things.

The Polar Bear, the Ringed Seal, and Three True Things

The polar bear waited patiently next to a hole in the sea ice. This was the breathing hole for a ringed seal, and a ringed seal meant a good meal for a hungry bear. It was only a matter of time before a seal would rise up to exhale and then take a gulp of fresh air. In the time it took the seal to breathe once or twice, the bear would lift that seal onto the ice and have herself a meal. She need only watch and wait.

Sure enough, in time a ringed seal poked his head out of the hole, and with one swipe of a mighty paw, the polar bear lifted him out of the water onto the ice.

"I beg you, please spare me," cried the seal. "I am old and tired and you are young and vigorous. Surely you can wait a little longer for a meal."

The bear paused. "You surprise me," she said. "You know the way of the world. Some must eat and some be eaten. However, I am inclined to let you live if you can think of three true things to tell me."

"And you will let me go?" asked the ringed seal.

"I promise," vowed the polar bear.

"Then here are three true things," proclaimed the ringed seal. "First, I wish that we had never met."

"Yes, I believe that is true," said the bear. "And the second true thing?"

"Second, I wish you had been blind when we did meet."

At this, the polar bear growled, but she had to admit it was doubtless true.

"But are you smart enough to offer a third true thing?" asked the bear.

"Oh, yes," said the ringed seal. "With all my heart, I can truly say I do not want to meet you ever again."

The polar bear turned her back to the seal and walked off along the vast sea ice. The ringed seal slipped back into the water, amazed at his release and eager to tell his story. But as true as his story of the three truths was, do you know that not a soul believed him!

Moral: Truth can be a powerful friend.

Author's Note

Aesop's fables number in the hundreds. "Fables" are stories told to teach particular lessons, stories which often conclude with a "moral"—a concise statement of the intended lesson. Animals are frequently the characters in fables, and in the weaknesses and strengths the animals exhibit in these stories, we can sometimes see ourselves.

Who was this Aesop credited with so many stories? We don't really know. The fables associated with him have been around for over a thousand years. Some say Aesop was a slave in Greece. Some say he was Ethiopian. He may not have been a real person at all; many different people may have composed these stories. Certainly, the stories were passed around long before anyone wrote them down.

Whoever Aesop might or might not have been, his name has been associated with hundreds of fables that have been told, retold, and remembered in countries all over the world. The stories in this collection are all based on Aesop's fables, but have been reimagined with the animals and geography of the Subarctic and Arctic regions of the globe.

About the Author

Susi Gregg Fowler's love of books was inevitable, with a grandmother who owned the bookstore in Juneau, Alaska, where Susi grew up and lives still. *Arctic Aesop's Fables* is her ninth children's book, and her poetry and essays for adults appear in national and regional journals and magazines. When she isn't writing, Susi enjoys making music, reading, hiking in the mountains around Juneau, traveling, and playing with her grandchildren.

About the Illustrator

Jim Fowler grew up in Tulsa, Oklahoma, and moved to Alaska in 1973. There he married Susi, a lifelong Alaskan, and they raised two daughters. *Arctic Aesop's Fables* is Jim's fourteenth children's book and the seventh he and Susi have created together. Jim divides his time between illustration and plein-air landscape painting. In 2010, he was awarded a Rasmuson Foundation Fellowship. Jim's earlier books include *Patsy Ann of Alaska* by Tricia Brown and *Benny's Flag* by Phyllis Krasilovsky.